Zalmoxis

Obscure Pagan

Lucian Blaga

Zalmoxis

Obscure Pagan

Translated by Doris Plantus-Runey
Introduction by Keith Hitchins

The Center for Romanian Studies

Las Vegas ◆ Chicago ◆ Palm Beach

Published in the United States of America by
Histria Books
7181 N. Hualapai Way, Ste. 130-86
Las Vegas, NV 89166 USA
HistriaBooks.com

The Center for Romanian Studies is an independent academic and cultural institute with the mission to promote knowledge of the history, literature, and culture of Romania in the world. The publishing program of the Center is affiliated with Histria Books. Contributions from scholars from around the world are welcome. To support the work of the Center for Romanian Studies, contact us at info@centerforromanianstudies.com

Library of Congress Control Number: 2019955246

ISBN 978-973-9432-17-7 (hardcover)
ISBN 978-1-59211-053-7 (paperback)
ISBN 978-1-59211-054-4 (eBook)

Contents

Zalmoxis
Obscure Pagan

Introduction

Lucian Blaga, who is judged by many to be Romania's most original philosopher and greatest poet of the twentieth century, is relatively little known in Western Europe and the English-speaking world. The reasons are not hard to find: he wrote in a language whose range was limited practically to a single country, and he represented a culture whose integration into Western European philosophical and literary currents was of comparatively recent origin. But in his own country he was a key figure in the intellectual and cultural life of the interwar period: he created a sublime poetry and constructed an intriguing philosophy of mystery; he made bold experiments in the drama; and he immersed himself in the great debate about Romanian national identity and paths of development. His accomplishments in each of these fields were exceptional, but his work, nonetheless, forms a whole. We cannot divide his philosophy, poetry, and drama into separate compartments, for the same metaphysical strivings and acute sensibility pervade all three.

I

Blaga was born on May 9, 1895 in the village of Lancrăm in southern Transylvania, where his father was the Orthodox parish priest. Impressions of his childhood spent in the village, a time of wonder and discovery by his own account, left powerful residues in his lyricism and his philosophy of culture. Although he left the village for the city to continue his education, he never ceased to draw inspiration from it as from an inexhaustible source of myth and metaphor.

He was attracted early to philosophy. His wide, but undirected readings while attending the Orthodox gymnasium in Braşov and the Orthodox Theological-Pedagogical Institute in Sibiu underwent channeling at the University of Vienna, where he studied during the latter years of the First World War. This sojourn in Vienna and shorter visits after the war deepened his attachment to certain currents of German philosophy, which he found congenial to his own probing of the nature of existence and of man's place in the cosmos. He had an enormous admiration for Goethe and Nietzsche. His experience of intellectual life in Vienna also confirmed his adherence to the "new style," or Expressionism, in literature, which he manifested in his first volumes of poetry.

The union of Transylvania, which had been part of the Austro-Hungarian Monarchy, with Romania at the end of the First World War brought a new orientation in Blaga's intellectual life. In a sense, he was drawn away from Vienna to Bucharest, the cultural as well as the political capital of Greater Romania. His creativity inevitably took new directions as he contributed unreservedly to the intellectual effervescence of interwar Romania. Yet, he shared with many of his colleagues the pervasive sense of spiritual unease in Romania and in Europe as a whole. Like intellectuals elsewhere, he was disillusioned with positivism and science and felt overwhelmed by the inability of reason to explain the deeper meaning of life. As he searched for permanent spiritual values he relied on an intuitive approach and an exploration of the irrational and the unconscious, although he never denied to reason and will an important role in his quest.

The interwar years were a time of intensive creativity for Blaga, a time when he produced the body of work that secured his place in Romanian letters. There were seven volumes of poetry, from *Poemele luminii* (The Poems of Light) in 1919 to *Nebănuitele trepte* (Unsuspected Steps) in 1943. In philosophy he began the construction of his system in the 1920s with "stages" such as his doctoral dissertation, *Cultura şi cunoştinţa* (Culture and Knowledge), which he defended at the University of Vienna in 1920. They were followed by the nine building blocks of the 1930s that formed the monumental trilogies: *Trilogia cunoaşterii* (The Trilogy of Knowledge) in 1943, *Trilogia culturii* (The Trilogy of Culture) in 1944, and *Trilogia valorilor* (The Trilogy of Values) in 1946. He also experimented with the drama, and his ten plays, from *Zamolxe* (Zalmoxis) in 1921 to *Arca lui Noe* (Noah's Ark) in 1944, ran the gamut from seemingly "folkloric" plays to Freudian dramas, to plays that sought to define the national character and understand man's creative vocation.

In the interwar period Blaga remained aloof from political struggle and did not become active on behalf of any major social cause. But he was by no means indifferent to the world around him. He wrote a constant stream of articles for newspapers and journals, usually on cultural questions and especially with reference to current and controversial issues. He also entered public service. In 1926 he accepted an appointment as press attaché at the Romanian legation in Warsaw, thus beginning a career in diplomacy that took him to similar posts in Prague, Belgrade, Bern, and Vienna, and culminated in his being named minister to Portugal in April 1938, a position he held until the following spring. Public honors also came to him. He was elected a member of the Romanian Academy in 1936, and in 1938 he was appointed to the chair of the philosophy of culture at the University of Cluj, a position created especially for him. For the next decade he used this unique forum to mold a new generation of intellectuals.

The normal course of academic life in Cluj and Blaga's own creative preoccupation were interrupted by the cession of northern Transylvania to Hungary in August 1940, a loss of territory and population forced upon Romania by Germany and Italy. Blaga was soon able to resume his work in Sibiu, where the University of Cluj had taken refuge. Besides teaching and writing, he founded and edited *Saeculum,* a review devoted to problems of philosophy, where he published essays of his own that were to form parts of new trilogies and welcomed the writings of others, even critics of his philosophical ideas. He also participated in a literary circle of gifted young writers and critics who, like him, were intent on giving Romanian literature a modern aesthetic and philosophical grounding. He returned to Cluj in 1945, following the expulsion of German and Hungarian armies from northern Transylvania.

Blaga was caught up in the great political and social ferment of the immediate postwar years, as the Romanian Communist Party, supported by the Soviet Union, whose troops occupied the country, gradually imposed a one-party dictatorship based on the Soviet model. In the educational and cultural institutions of the new regime there was no room for men like Blaga. In 1948 he was removed from the University of Cluj and the Romanian Academy and, in effect, reduced to silence. Although he continued to write poetry and elaborate his philosophical system, neither of these activities was congenial to the new order and were works, as he himself put it, intended for the desk drawer. Except for translations, notably Goethe's *Faust* in 1955 and Lessing's *Nathan the Wise* in 1956, he published little of his own work until the last year of his life, when a few poems and short newspaper articles appeared. He died on May 6, 1961 in Cluj from cancer.

In the 1960s a reevaluation of Blaga's work got under way. As the Communist Party placed increasing emphasis on the national culture, new editions of his poetry and, later, of his philosophical works were published, and literary critics and historians undertook searching investigations of his work and life. The fall of the Communist regime in 1989 removed the remaining ideological constraints on the treatment of his philosophical and aesthetic ideas and led to comprehensive critical assessments of his place in Romanian letters.

II

Blaga occupies a singular place in the history of Romanian philosophy. Because of the problems and the methods that preoccupied him, he stood apart from his Romanian contemporaries. Engrossed in his own original pursuit of the absolute, he undertook to elucidate the nature of being and to discover the meaning of existence in ways other than those belonging to the philosophical tradition of his own country. He was, rather, indebted to European sources, and he regarded himself as belonging to the tradition of European thought that had its origins in Classical Greece.

Blaga shared the leading ideas of that great turn in European thought that occurred m the 1890s. Like Freud, Bergson, and others, who were its harbingers, and however much he might differ with them in detail, he accepted their general proposition that the ultimate foundation of human activity lay elsewhere than in logical thinking and that knowledge isolated from non-logical influences was impossible. Yet, like them, he could not dispense with reason and used the accepted methods of rational argument in explaining his own theories of cosmic and human development. Even so, he was forever dissatisfied with the explanations of man's condition set forth by nineteenth-century rationalism.

Foremost among the sources from which he drew in constructing his own system was German philosophy. His debt to Goethe, the German Romantics, and Nietzsche was immense, and he readily acknowledged it. He warmly praised Goethe and was one of the few philosophers of the time to take his experiments in the natural sciences seriously. He was impressed especially by Goethe's ability to contemplate natural phenomena from a perspective of spatial and temporal wholeness, and he, too, sought the *Urphänomen,* or primordial phenomenon, which elucidated the nature of entire cultures and civilizations. He may also have owed to Goethe his aversion to the sort of rationalistic analysis, which, he thought, rather than illuminating its object, pulverized it. As for the German Romantics, they turned his thought to myth and metaphysics and led him into those vague, secluded regions where his creative imagination could soar. From Nietzsche he learned to appreciate cultural style and to question established spiritual values, and thus it is impossible to study Blaga's writings on the philosophy of culture without being struck by the similarity to Nietzsche's mode of thought or to read Blaga's play *Zamolxe* without feeling the presence of Zarathustra.

At the heart of Blaga's philosophy was his eagerness to grasp the meaning of existence and to discover man's role in the universe. In his quest he confronted directly the great enigmas that obscured man's destiny and accepted the unknown for what it was: a mystery that could never be fully revealed. Indeed, mystery was the fundamental category of his philosophy in the same way that the "idea" was for Plato or the "category" for Kant. Blaga's world was saturated with mysteries of all kinds, and he lamented that philosophers had neglected or shunned altogether the idea of mystery. For him mystery was not the completely unknowable but an obscurity not yet adequately illuminated. It was full of meaning precisely because it concealed so much, and this overpowering incitement to investigation led Blaga to the depths of the human psyche and to the farthest limits of human reason.

As for man's place in the cosmos, Blaga showed no hesitation in assigning him to the horizon of mystery. In the trilogies he insisted that man's vocation could be none other than to reveal mystery and that, in so doing, he became a creator of culture. All these things, Blaga argued, had been determined ontologically: man was a creator of culture simply because he was man, because he belonged to a mode of existence that was exclusively human.

Blaga judged his own role as a philosopher from this perspective. As a metaphysician he took it as his duty to create a world of his own and confessed that if he failed to do so, he would consider his vocation unfulfilled. He was thus intent upon penetrating the mystery of existence, but he harbored no illusions about the truth that such an endeavor might bring forth. He was certain that the attainment of ultimate truth was beyond man's capability because the limitations on his knowledge of the absolute were inherent in his very mode of existence. Truth, then, in the usual meaning of the term, could not, Blaga concluded in *Trilogia cunoaşterii,* be the object of the creative act. Instead, he proposed attainable goals such as "the possible," "the imaginable," and "the beautiful." Even so, he recognized the supreme dignity of the human spirit in striving to know the unknowable, and he insisted that it took the place of divine revelation in exposing, in however fragmentary a fashion, the nature of being.

Blaga was intrigued by how man approached the unknowable, that is, by what mechanisms he created culture, and thus he was led to investigate cultural style. By the term style he did not mean the outward form of a work of art or literature but rather its manner of being. It was style, he argued in *Trilogia culturii,* that imbued works of art and literature and even entire ethnic communities and historical periods with their unique character; it was style that revealed the hidden side of human nature and thus became the principal means of objectifying human spirituality; and it was style that caused creativity to differ from individual to individual, people to people, and period to period.

Besides mystery, the unconscious was an indispensable component of Blaga's theory of style. Indeed, he located the source of style in (he unconscious, and, thus, his theory of style and his entire philosophy of culture were based on the proposition that creative acts such as the structuring of a work of art, a philosophical theory, or a scientific hypothesis were directed by powers beyond the control of the conscious. As he put it, style was the "supreme yoke" which held an author, a current, or an entire culture in bondage and from which none could escape. Although he did not question the important contribution that the conscious made to the external elaboration of style, he denied that man's fundamental way of being, his "inner style," could be substantially altered by his own will.

Blaga took issue with those who dismissed the unconscious as a zone of primitive, animal impulses devoid of true creativity or as a kind of basement of the conscious to which a multitude of suppressed or unwanted emotions had been consigned. On the contrary, he argued, the unconscious was a psychic reality possessing its own "sovereign" functions and an internal order and equilibrium of unlimited creative virtues. He admired Jung especially for having enriched the doctrine of the unconscious through his theory psychic archetypes, which Blaga adapted for his own conception of the unconscious categories, and through his theory of the collective unconscious, which helped Blaga to account for the continuity of cultural style through the centuries.

Blaga endowed the unconscious with a series of categories, which, structurally, resembled Kant's categories of the conscious. They were the determinants of style and, grouped together, they formed a general pattern, or "stylistic matrix," which imposed itself on every culture and endowed it with individuality. The primary and secondary categories of the matrix were capable of infinite combinations, which were thus responsible for the myriad variations of cultural style.

Blaga was fascinated not only by the theoretical aspects of style, but eagerly undertook to apply his ideas to Romanian culture, explaining its uniqueness by using the categories of the unconscious stylistic matrix. He concentrated on the rural world, where he thought the main constituent elements of Romanian spirituality lay. He conceived of the Romanian village as the locale of the organic, preeminently human mode of existence, the place where the generating sources of the native culture were strongest and purest. In fact, when he spoke of "culture" he meant the creative life of the village, and it was through this culture, "our eternity revealed in time," that the Romanians participated in the great adventure of cosmic creation. He contrasted this culture, a product of the "rural soul," with "civilization," whose embodiment was the city, the mechanized, bourgeois world, whose collapse seemed to him close at hand. For him, the great urban center of the twentieth century was the locale of "non-creative" preoccupations such as the accumulation of positive knowledge and the formulation of nationalistic conceptions; it was the place where man lost his "cosmic sentiment" and his attachment to the specifically human, organic mode of existence. But the village was for him always the preeminent zone of mythical thought, which assimilated concrete appearances and enabled man to enter into a creative relationship with existence.

III

Blaga's poetic craft evolved under the aegis of European modernism, especially of those poetic movements in the early decades of the century in Germany and Austria usually grouped together as Expressionism. He shared with the Expressionists and others the idea of poetry as an adventure in cognition, as an activity of the self-examining mind. Like them, he was continually reflecting upon the significance of the poetic act and translating his meditations into verse of profound metaphysical sensibility and beauty. Like them, too, he was distrustful of unbridled inspiration and personal exultation. Indeed, he thought of himself as a builder, as one who followed Apollo rather than Dionysus, who prized conscious creation, and whose occasional transports of enthusiasm never descended into chaos.

Of all the varied currents of creative ideas Blaga sampled in the early stages of his poetic career, German Expressionism was undoubtedly the most irresistible. He wrote about it with obvious enthusiasm, and it formed the basis of his theory and art of poetry in the 1920s. Expressionist aesthetics gave meaning and direction to his artistic aspirations and reinforced his longing to attain the absolute and his passionate search for the essence of life. He felt a close kinship with those Expressionists who were made desperate by a sense of isolation from ordinary humanity, and, like them, he attributed the condition to an exaggerated intellectualism that numbed the ability to behave and feel normally. Together they found solace in Bergson's theory of the *élan vital,* which postulated an unceasing conflict between the inhibiting intellect and the unconscious flow of life, and they were anxious to return to some primordial form of existence when everything was feeling and stood in close communion with nature. Blaga also shared the spiritual despair of the Expressionists, who took literally Nietzsche's pronouncement that God was dead, and in his own poetry he strove to create an ideal world to answer the fundamental questions of existence.

The connection between Blaga's poetry and philosophy is evident, and Blaga himself insisted that his poetic expression could never be solely a spontaneous act of sensibility or inspiration, but had to be molded also by his metaphysical speculations. His preoccupation with philosophy is so manifest that no special effort to prove philosophical influences on his poetry is necessary. Yet, his poetry is not simply a more lyrical expression of his philosophy, and he himself denied that his poetry was merely one of ideas or was in some way didactic. Although a knowledge of his philosophical system is not required for an appreciation of his poetry, nonetheless, a recognition of the great metaphors of his philosophy — the Great Anonymous One, luciferian cognition, and transcendental censorship — and an understanding of his theory of mystery enrich the spiritual background against which he projects his poetic visions.

The first poem of Blaga's first volume, *Poemele luminii,* laid the foundation of his vision of the world. The opening line, "I do not crush the world's corolla of wonder," expresses his intuition of cosmic life as being present in all things and his belief that all animate beings and inanimate objects share in the secret of eternity. In these postulates he discovers the meaning of human existence and recognizes his duty to pursue the unknown to its ultimate source. He expresses dissatisfaction with appearances and is persuaded that true reality exists in a magic substance which pervades the entire world of phenomena. This absolute essence, he insists, reveals itself to those who will be guided not by the mind, which destroys the secret of things, but by "holy mystery," which enriches even the darkest horizons of existence.

Blaga's cosmic vision does not admit of easy generalizations, but at the heart of it lies an essentially animist conception. Together with the idea of mystery it is fundamental to the nature of his poetry. In *Trilogia culturii* he argued that every aspect of reality, every motion, from the fluttering of a leaf to the falling of a ray of sunlight, participated in the joy and suffering of man. This inanimate world was nothing less than an extension of the human body; when the branch of a tree stirred man felt its swaying like a gesture of his arm, or he could feel light as a resurrection and colors as joyfulness.

Confronted by a world whose essences were the unknown and the impenetrable, Blaga pursued its infinite secrets undaunted. The reality he strove to understand was filled with contradictions that defied reason and logic. It became for him a region not of the irrational but of the non-rational, where human intelligence could operate only at the intuitive level. This was the region he called "mystery." His poetic universe, as well as his philosophical system, ultimately turn on this major metaphor. The same metaphysics of mystery, which pervades the trilogies, is mirrored in his volumes of poetry. Yet, as we have seen, he did not write poems to illustrate his philosophy. Rather, he was responding to a deep lyrical calling.

Blaga's poetic approach to mystery took The form of mythic thinking. Indeed, he could not conceive of a poetry divorced from myth, for he believed it to be the only means of penetrating beyond mere logical appearances to the essence of things. Myth was a way of expressing intuited truths, of putting into words and images presentiments and ideas that could not be precisely formulated. He was convinced that certain realities could be dealt with more effectively through the "mythic method," or "mythosophy," than by scientific, logical analysis.

Another of Blaga's devices for penetrating Mystery was metaphor. He was certain that the hidden aspects of existence made themselves known through metaphor, which tabled man to gain at least a glimpse of reality. The metaphor performed a function similar to that of mythic thinking by piercing those zones that were closed to reason. Both operated on the "edge of reason" where meaning could only be intuited and communicated obliquely. In Blaga's conception, therefore, metaphor and myth possessed crucial cognitive virtues through their ability to establish striking, original relations between things which in isolation would have little or no deeper significance.

Blaga combined restless philosophical inquiry with a delicate poetic sensibility to produce a unique body of work. In so doing, he made crucial contributions to Romanian poetry. He applied myth on a scale not seen before, and his boldness in using free verse in his early volumes helped to establish it as the dominant form of modern Romanian prosody.

IV

At about the time Blaga published his first volumes of poems and his first essays in the philosophy of culture he completed work on his first play, *Zamolxe* (Zalmoxis), his so-called "Dacian drama." Its appearance in 1921 was mainly a response to artistic and philosophical preoccupations that had already manifested themselves in two books of poetry, *Poemele lummii* in 1919 and *Paşii profetului* (The Footsteps of the Prophet) in 1921, and in *Cultura şi cunoştinţa.*

Blaga turned to the drama, first of all, to satisfy his own creative aspirations. As a poet he was constantly testing new forms, and now he was eager to try his hand at the dramatic poem. He had already included several in *Paşii profetului,* and he intended *Zamolxe* to be his most ambitious experiment to date with the genre. As a philosopher he was eager to pursue his investigation of the mystery of existence and to deepen his understanding of cultural style. He was intrigued especially by the complexities of the Romanian cultural style and the apparent contradictions in its spiritual manifestations. He set forth his ideas on the subject in an article, "Revolta fondului nostru nelatin" (The Revolt of Our Non-Latin Sources), published in the same year as *Zamolxe.* In it he insisted that the Romanians were much more than Latins with their clarity, rationality, and classical sense of balance. He pointed out that even though Latinity predominated, the Romanians also had a rich Slavic-Dacian heritage, exuberant and full of life, which from time forced its way into the Romanian consciousness. This revolt of their non-Latin sources, originating in the "metaphysical depths" of the Romanian spirit, violently disturbed its Latin symmetry and harmony and proved the infinite diversity of the Romanian cultural style. Blaga found himself powerfully drawn to the Dacians, one of the ancestors of the Romanians who had been conquered by the Romans, because they appealed to his poetic sensibilities: he viewed their world as overflowing with vitality, open to nature, and yearning for the absolute.

Blaga chose Zamolxe as the hero of his play because he seemed to epitomize all that the Dacians represented spiritually. He was, to be sure, an historical figure. According to the ancient Greeks, Zalmoxis, as he was known, had been a Dacian slave to the philosopher Pythagoras on the island of Samos who had acquired great knowledge from his master and who had returned to the Dacians, bringing them the religious teachings he had assimilated. Among the Dacians he was a priest and prophet, and under the name Gebeleizis he was also a celestial deity. A cult developed around him, and temples were dedicated to his memory, one of which recalled the place to which he was said to have retired every three years to meditate.

In portraying his hero, Blaga drew on the information provided by ancient and modern historians, but *Zamolxe* is not an historical drama. Rather, Blaga was intent on exploring the most remote layers of Romanian spirituality, and he was guided by his imagination and his lyric sensibility. He put himself in the figure of Zamolxe, and thus the portrait of the Dacian prophet that emerges is a self-portrait. It is Blaga, disguised as Zamolxe, who confronts the mystery of existence and seeks the meaning of cultural style and who tests hypotheses that will reach their fullest expression later in the trilogies.

Zamolxe is divided into three acts of three scenes each, which introduce the principal characters — Zamolxe, the High Priest, and the Dacians — and depict their relations with one another. In composition the play resembles a poem, as Blaga chooses to reveal his characters through monologues and dialogues rather than through action. The main conflict is one of ideas between Zamolxe and the High Priest, who are at odds over how men shall relate to the world. The High Priest, who resides in the city, stands for the old order, the traditional polytheistic faith, which has become institutionalized and has separated the Dacians from nature, while Zamolxe, who lives close to nature and shuns the city, represents a new beginning, a religion that will reconcile the Dacians with their true essence. Blaga's attachment to Expressionist ideals is discernible in his treatment of the characters primarily as vehicles of ideas and his preference for primitive nature over the cultured metropolis.

The play opens with Zamolxe seated in front of a cave contemplating nature and feeling himself a part of nature and touching the mystery of existence. He had taken refuge there seven years earlier when the people had driven him from the city where he had preached a new religion, that of the Great Blind Man. At first, solitude had been congenial to him, but now he is ready to return to his people to share with them the wisdom he has acquired in seven years of meditation. Although he feels a duty to undertake this mission, he hesitates because it is contrary to his contemplative nature. As he thus stands between two worlds, one of reflection and the other of deeds, three visions appear to him one after the other: Socrates, Jesus, and Giordano Bruno. The message they bring him is an admonition to take action, but their fate as prophets reinforces his presentiment of tragedy. Yet, in the end, he decides to leave the cave and return to the world of men.

Zamolxe's mission to his people occurs at a time of spiritual crisis among the Dacians: the old gods are dead, as men have ceased to believe in them, and a reevaluation of all values is under way. Despite his banishment, Zamolxe's teachings have steadily gained ground among the people, and the old ecclesiastical order is threatened with dissolution as the people revolt and try to seize the temple and depose the High Priest. But the High Priest is resourceful. He spreads the word that Zamolxe is a god who descended among men to teach them youth and suffering. Calm immediately returns to the city, and the populace asks the High Priest to place a statue of Zamolxe in the temple alongside the other gods. This he does only too gladly because he hopes to blunt Zamolxe's message by associating him with the old gods.

In the meantime, Zamolxe has arrived at a meadow outside the city. When he learns that he has been made a god, he rushes to the temple to challenge the High Priest. Zamolxe throws down his statue, and the people, who do not recognize him, kill him with pieces of his own statue. Both Zamolxe and his teachings have seemingly perished, but the Dacians have a sudden revelation of the presence among them and in them of the Great Blind Man, the revelation that Blaga refers to in the designation of his play as a "pagan mystery."

The central figure of the play is Zamolxe. It is he to whom all the other figures are connected, and it is he who, in essence, defines them. He is also the most complex of the figures, a contemplative and melancholic being who savors solitude, but who is also a reformer driven by a sense of mission to bring about a spiritual rebirth of his people. There are obvious similarities between Zamolxe and Christ, but they are superficial: Zamolxe was not a divinity, nor was his revelation divine. I here are also similarities between Zamolxe and Nietzsche's superman, but Zamolxe is not Zarathustra. Even though Zamolxe's dispute with the High Priest, his attacks on the traditional gods, and his efforts to prepare men to accept new values are reminiscent of Zarathustra's diatribes against the priests and attacks on all that was outmoded, Zamolxe was a gentler, more human figure who remained attached to the common people.

Through Zamolxe's sacrifice the Dacians rise above their immediate, primitive impulses, which were frenzied and wanton. As Zamolxe had taught them, the religion of the Great Blind Man symbolized the fusion of nature and the divine and was the embodiment of the creative, if sometimes aimless, power of nature. In embracing it, they cast aside the gods that the High Priest had set up between them and nature. They became themselves, that is, they returned to the deep, unconscious sources of their faith, symbolized by a serene communion with nature.

Keith Hitchins

Translator's Foreword.

The eloquence of Lucian Blaga's play *Zamolxe, mister pagan,* is its earnest attempt at fording an imposing barrier that separated a Latinized people from a dissociated non-Roman past. Recorded by Herodotus in his *Histories,* and since sustained by oral tradition, Zalmoxis is reported to have been a prophet-priest to a branch of the Thracian people called Getae by Greek writers, and Dacian by the Romans. The Thracians were an extensive tribe stretching from the north of Greece throughout the Balkans, with the Dacians occupying the Danube basin in present day Romania. Although Zalmoxis persists historically in an opaque light as an obscure, passionate hero in the orphic tradition, Blaga openly creates a myth that speaks to the complex and innovative religion of the Thracians at that time: the concept of immortality. He germinates the historical component of Zalmoxis into a mythical persona in order to explore the substance of the myth, thus the story of the enigmatic prophet-priest possesses little more than the invariant core conceived by ancient Dacians in terms of factual content in Blaga's play. Herodotus, after all, identifies Zalmoxis as the god of the Dacian religion, whose central tenet was immortality. Beyond that, *Zalmoxis* is pure Blaga.

The dynamics of translating a work that in its own heart remains conflicted with issues of cultural transmission and autochthony presented curious challenges on several levels. Fortunately, Lucian Blaga is remarkable as a writer for his ability to reconcile poetical and philosophical arrays of reasonable inference. The latitude for convergent meaning is generous; the focus of Blaga's myth has a built-in inevitability that allows the task of translation to operate within very stable territory. Therefore, despite a Nabokovian temptation to render the real work over a cosmetic embellishment, I focused on the inherent relativity between characters, plot, and theme, while aiming at "transposing" the three-dimensional attributes of language. For practical purposes I strove to translate the first draft in a Ciceronian style before exploiting cultural and historical associations of individual words and phrases. I tried leaving as few of my fingerprints as possible for as many times as I turned words over (and over). Romanian — the source language — is replete with more than two thousand years of culture, folklore, history, and as many mysteries as Orpheus and Dionysus combined, since linguistic and historical evidence make the point that its origins include a significant non-Latin root.

The translatability of the text revealed just how pertinent translation theory was to a play whose action is both spatially and temporally remote. Blaga undertook to translate a significant historical and folkloric component of an indigenous culture without the luxury of knowing the ancient source language. In, he was attempting to access a non-Roman ancestral culture via a Latinized people and language. It is not the present concern of this translation to speculate on the political implications of Blaga's intentions, although they are exquisitely present; such integral properties of the play make for fertile discussions in their own right. It is worth noting, however, that such issues of national identity and cultural birthright contribute heavily to the dynamics of the play proper. Part of the myth-making process is, finally, a matter of inning, arrangement, and purpose. Not only does Blaga create *Zamolxe* as a myth; he does it in a contemporary language of Zalmoxis' posterity — a correctly anticipated maneuver. The fact that he extends an ancient culture to what would be its natural endpoint reflects Blaga's perception of language as subject to forces of evolution. He manages, hence, to create also a sense of syncretized strangeness in contemporary Romanian by reinforcing key aspects of oral tradition, not limited to remote metaphor, complex imagery, and extremely inert semiotics. For example, Herodotus tells us that Zalmoxis preached immortality and at some point sequestered himself in a cave for four years before returning among his people. Blaga invents the circumstances that shape his play at great risk, no doubt. But he succeeds in providing stunning, yet subtle insight into aspects of dionysiac and orphic mysteries, as well. Even in its source language, translatability becomes an issue, insofar as it must depart from the vertical and horizontal axis of theoreticians, and operate within a cultural continuum that has a Möebius feature to it. For this reason, I contemplated translation as the first intent of conveyance, even when functioning within a single language system. By way of illustration, Blaga must translate a distant culture from an unknown ancestral language via the account of Herodotus and others. The source language is virtually embedded in the vague but authenticated documentation of a real figure. I might agree that it is quite impossible to convey the entirety of one meaning into another language, but not even language can do this in capturing a sense from non-utterance to utterance.

Rather, everything is a series of conveyances whose sole objective is not merely to inform the subtleties of myth but sustain them as well, through language. In other words, within the limits of a musical scale that permits twelve pitches, and only twelve, octaves of the same note produce a different "sound" in terms of frequency and timbre. So, too, with translating.

Consequently, I solved what struck me as a problematic passage in Zalmoxis' opening monologue, and again in the end of Act III, by creating an internal dialogue. Although a risky stylistic transposition, I tried to converge upon Blaga's meaning a better translation of that which Zalmoxis was attempting to convey. Since this is a spoken part, the length in pure translation would be far too heavy on a Western audience. Likewise, the relationship Blaga is trying to feature between Zalmoxis and nature would be difficult to tease out of such dense language. I introduced, therefore, the voice of Zalmoxis as an aspect of his orphic/dionysiac emblem so that the audience has immediate access to a crucial concern in the play, without the monotony of a monologue. But this bold device is less a departure from I he invariant core, than a convergence upon it.

By translating *Zamolxe* into English, I l hope to offer Western scholarship a refreshing work of extraordinary possibilities vis-a-vis traditional classics such as *The Bacchae,* by Euripides. Blaga's work reveals healthy contrasts to traditional views of tragedy, irony, mysteries, death, and myth. It provides a different vantage point, relative to character, structure, and theme from which to perceive and redefine our discriminating approach to literature.

I owe a tremendous debt of gratitude to Dr. Anca Vlasopolos for her meticulous guidance, enthusiasm, and genuine understanding of the craft of translation. Most of all I express my appreciation for her tacit urging to do what I love. I want also to thank Lucian Vasilie for his advice and encouragement, and for his insight into all things Thracian.

Doris Plantus-Runey

For Benjamin and Daniel,
pui de traci

Zalmoxis

Obscure Pagan

Cast of Characters

ZALMOXIS Young charismatic prophet

MAGUL An old priest SORCERER

WOODCARVER A Greek

ZEMORA Daughter of Magul

SHEPHERD

HUNCHBACK

THREE APPARITIONS:

OLD MAN

YOUNG MAN

MAN ON THE STAKE

CHILDREN:

THE SMALLEST CHILD

THE MIDDLE CHILD

THE OLDEST CHILD

SOLDIERS

DACIAN PEOPLE

The play takes place in the mountains of the Dacian people, cc. 1 BC.

Act I

Scene 1

A large cave entrance. Many rocks. Dusk. An old hollowed oak tree. Zalmoxis with a deer skin about his shoulders sits on a rock at the mouth of the cave.

ZALMOXIS

(alone)

A lake calmed by days without wind am I, and I am alone, so alone that I cannot tell where I end and all that surrounds me begins. Man to man are you; you... and I. Nothing is strange to me, and I lack only the sea. So I take communion with each drop of all that grows and does not perish.

My spirit has spread here his mighty cloak – my spirit and the spirit of the world is one and the same as much —

(addressing his spirit in nature)

we are as man to man, "you... and I."

(redirecting his address)

But for all the times he is silent, and the times he sings not, he waits; he waits and the good dream comes to caress him once more.

(the sound of crickets)

Man to man, you... and I. Loneliness washes away boundaries, and lets you braid yourself with nature's secrets until you lose yourself in the rock and run off in waves, into the ground.

(silence)

Am I turning inward, or stretching my ear to the forest?

(shriek of a blackbird)

Is it God?

Is it the Blind One?

(crickets again)

So distant are my Dacian people, brother of the bear.

(redirecting his address to his people)

You mistook my purpose and struck at my words with stones when I tried to bring you a new and robust religion from the heart of the Unknown One. There was a time when I howled. I wanted to raise even the mountains in mutiny against you. And I called to them: Tumble down your madness and heave waters over my proud Thracian people.

But it's a long time since then; today my venom has subsided; a bedrock of wisdom has set itself down.

VOICE OF ZALMOXIS

The sun had sent forth all of its honey in the orchards when first you spoke the parable.

(Zalmoxis reflects)

— You cannot speak of God but in this way, you told them. You embody him in a flower and raise him in your palms —

ZALMOXIS

—you conceive him in your mind and make him secret in your soul —

VOICE OF ZALMOXIS

— you perceive him a wellspring, and you let him run gently over your feet...

ZALMOXIS

...you make him... the sun and gather him with your eyes, you imagine him a man and invite him to your village —

VOICE OF ZALMOXIS

— where all of mankind's dreams await him.

ZALMOXIS

You scatter grains between the furrows and you say:

VOICE OF ZALMOXIS

From these grains grow God.

On that morning, so that even the children could understand me, I changed you into a blind man. I told them "we are the seeing"—

VOICE OF ZALMOXIS

— while God is an old blind man.

ZALMOXIS

Each one of us is his child, and each one takes him by the hand. For are you not all powerful? The mysterious Blind One who feels his way among the thorns? You know not from whence you come, nor where you are going. You are the tormented thought crushed to nothing. You writhe eternally, finding a way —

VOICE OF ZALMOXIS

— to make miracles as they were never made before —

ZALMOXIS

But your arms are not as strong as your dream is lofty. So often do you fall never once thinking it was the storm from the light you created. Do you cry out to me? Me? Do you call me?

VOICE OF ZALMOXIS

From the bottom of the sea, your turbulent cry comes... comes.

ZALMOXIS

Behold, I am your creation and here are your eyes. Do you want them?

VOICE OF ZALMOXIS

Are you not to take your fate upon your small shoulders without coercion?

ZALMOXIS

...Oh, powerful Blind One.

Quiet one, sad one, we your saviors, we, wild children. Why did they mangle my mouth with stones when thus I spoke of you that morning? Was the sun not kind enough?

And didn't my thoughts frighten the birds from the trees.

(gentle sound of birds)

VOICE OF ZALMOXIS

Since then so much time has been confounded...

ZALMOXIS

...the abyss has soothed my bitterness with its rays. Here are the rambling silences through which you can see the back of the world.

He rises and removes a golden honeycomb from the hollow of an oak tree. He wrings it out, and the honey drips in the sand.

ZALMOXIS

Oh, new autumn!

My hive is full and its honey drizzles off the lips like milk that oozes from the lips of a babe who has sucked to much.

From now on the evenings will become much colder, one after the other, from each oak leaf, a brass bell, while at night many stars will fall. I will stay at the mouth of the cave and number them in silence. I will say to myself "the stars are turning earthward!"

But will my steps find the way to the fortress as they spark against the flint? Will I find my way to the world?

VOICE OF ZALMOXIS

Smiling in the temple they will scatter many seeds for the doves of God.

Zalmoxis retreats into the cave.

Scene 2

The walls of the fortress can be seen in the distance. On the left is a part of the temple, columns and stairs all around. In the front of the temple somewhat behind are gallows. Sunset. The soldiers guard the temples, they huddle in a pile, only one is standing on the steps with his spear on his shoulder. Two workers are late with the last touches on the gallows.

A SOLDIER

(speaking to the foreign soldier)

Where did our people capture you?

FOREIGN SOLDIER

Near the Danube.

ANOTHER SOLDIER

Don't you miss your country?

FOREIGN SOLDIER

Oh, yes. Where I come from the oranges grow with the red fruit, the gods don't have oxen with horns like those you raise, and in the winter, the snowflakes don't swarm. By us, it's altogether different, except the sun seems so much like this one — you'd think they were one in the same!

(all laugh)

THE FIRST SOLDIER

You're the first slave who rejoices over a liberated life on these plains. Why, you have the same rights as we do. We didn't know your long-suffering master, though. Tell us, how did you win your freedom?

FOREIGN SOLDIER

(cunningly)

With... the prophet's slippers...

ALL

With what? Come on, tell us the story!

FOREIGN SOLDIER

How long have you chased Zalmoxis?

THE FIRST SOLDIER

A few years.

FOREIGN SOLDIER

That's good. His servants are working hard underground, like rabbits in the yard. Otherwise why would we be watching the temple day and night? Magul is terrified of their power. He has even promised to make a wild gift of his daughter to the one who will uncover Zalmoxis' trail. Or have you forgotten?

THE SECOND SOLDIER

Ah-ha! The provocative Zemora. Who doesn't desire her!

FOREIGN SOLDIER

(smiling cajolingly)

I was living a pathetic life. Even the dogs felt sorry for me. So I decided to seek out the hidden Zalmoxis. I searched through the mountains, pushed myself for nine days through ravines and in the end I found nothing but a pair of slippers. These must belong to Zalmoxis, I thought to myself, so I made a gift of them to the priest. It's true, I only brought the slippers and not the head of the prophet, but even that should have been worth one night with Zemora. But Magul is cheap. He gave me only this rag — of liberty. Yesterday he asked me when I would bring him the head of Zalmoxis and I told him "When he will lose it as he lost his slippers, your holiness!

SOLDIER ON WATCH

(standing)

A polite response, indeed, but you should have remained a slave instead of guarding the temple with heathens like us; and our heels grow fat on these holy stones since our faith has left us. Where are those days when the sound of the trumpet aimed toward the sun, and through the flaxen stubble our arrows flew between the horns of oxen?

THE THIRD SOLDIER

And the catfish we pulled from the brooks were as round as the calves of maidens.

THE FOURTH SOLDIER

(to the soldier of the watch)

Look at how the hang noose sways in the wind.

THE FIFTH SOLDIER

Patience, children, patience. Don't grumble. When the enemy moves about we will send such a howling to the sea that Magul will forget about his altars.

SOLDIER ON WATCH

Guess my riddle, boys: there are beings that are not real, yet a man perceives in them danger! Why? So that very man can beg help of them in times of danger...

THE SEVENTH SOLDIER

Your riddle is a beast to understand.

THE EIGHTH SOLDIER

On the contrary. These are gods.

THE FIRST SOLDIER

And still we watch over them and keep thieves at bay with our spears.

SOLDIER ON WATCH

And they aren't even real! Ha Ha!

THE SECOND SOLDIER

(to the soldier on watch)

Aren't you, too, one of Zalmoxis' "blind ones?"

THE THIRD SOLDIER

Quiet! Magul is coming out of the altar.

Everyone assembles into two lines. Magul walks among the spears and looks with agile eyes.

MAGUL

The ravens want to see pitchforks at dawn. Did you understand? At night, spare no one.

He disappears in the back of the temple. The soldiers bow and take their places.

THE FOURTH SOLDIER

The high priest has a such a piercing look, he can see into your thoughts.

THE FIFTH SOLDIER

The old Mag! He left with his daughter when the cocks were still singing. When he returned much later, he was alone. The fury of the Blind One is great, and she is, after all, so beautiful, you would think he'd have hidden her like a treasure somewhere far away in the mountains.

THE SIXTH SOLDIER

People say he never sleeps.

THE SEVENTH SOLDIER

He has the eyes of a wolf in the dark that glow like embers in the wind.

THE EIGHTH SOLDIER

(mysteriously)

Magul is silent.

THE NINTH SOLDIER

Magul is cold.

THE FIRST SOLDIER

Steadfast as a custom left by our forefathers.

THE SECOND SOLDIER

Bloodthirsty as a beast.

SOLDIER ON WATCH

(bursting in)

More than a beast. Bloodthirsty as the holy lessons of today and all times.

FOREIGN SOLDIER

How red is the sky...

THE FOURTH SOLDIER

...and the gallows are ready.

FOREIGN SOLDIER

(looking toward the temple)

My friends, a dreadful night awaits us — look there! A tom cat — a bad sign.

THE FIFTH SOLDIER

A torn cat with green eyes like Magul. Catch him! Catch him — tie his carcass to the pitchfork with a rope and frighten all the rebels.

SOLDIER ON WATCH

(bursts out laughing and turns back toward the temple)

Ha-ha! O gods, moldy with eternity! Is there not one tight fist to smash the lie with stone columns? Maybe among the dead. Come out, you who've been buried alive, and you, who have been cast upon rivers. I, one of Zalmoxis' remaining faithful summon you forth from the deep. I am the man — ha-ha — Lay siege to the sanctuary!

O, gods, shielded with strangled kittens, I am disgusted.

(He throws a spear into the gates of the temple and bows.)

I salute you!

(The others quickly jump him and beat him down with their spear handles.)

Scene 3

A sorcerer's cottage. Night. Fire burns in the hearth. The flames light up the inside. The sorcerer wears Thracian horns. He takes from a corner a human skull, and fills it with wine from a jug. Loud pounding is heard at the door, and he sets the skull down on the hearth.

SORCERER

Who is it?

A VOICE

Magul.

The sorcerer opens the door. Magul enters panting.

MAGUL

Give me shelter beneath the roof of your power. Not from thunder, but from the bulls. Zalmoxis' disciples have risen up. Word travels through the fortress that the brook awaits me this night.

SORCERER

And the temples?

MAGUL

The hearty soldiers keep watch over it.

SORCERER

Hearty they may be, but are they faithful as well?

MAGUL

As faithful as the smoke from incense.

Magul grows quiet.

SORCERER

Has Zalmoxis returned?

MAGUL

Since he has run away, they have not discovered his tracks. Some say that he has become a lonely wretch in the mountains, but others whisper that he will surely come again and snatch the temple away from me, and smash the idols.

SORCERER

A prophet is nothing, but an injured prophet is much. It has been exactly seven years since you directed the people to cast him out. I didn't advise you, and here you are.

MAGUL

(disgusted)

People, people!

SORCERER

How holy would his madness be were it not so fickle.

MAGUL

(despairing)

My heart is bitter with questions. The gods — how will we escape them? I am the keeper of eternity — how will we lose them? Must I fall?

SORCERER

The gods thrive on the soul of man. When this nutrient has been depleted, when all cease to believe in them anymore, they gather sadly And call for their own end. Neither honey nor goat's milk can help them.

MAGUL

(raising his hands)

O, ye undead. Your faithlessness dries you up, your salvation blinks from nowhere. For years have

I tossed restlessly, and in vain, for not even the black tablets of wisdom brought out of Egypt gave me the answer. Not even the Siren's recollection of advice heard in the smoke at Delphi.

SORCERER

Not even the highest of virtues?

MAGUL

(collecting his thoughts)

Deceit?

SORCERER

The eternal spring of advice. Come, calm yourself. The answer you seek will have to knock on your door one day — if not today, then tomorrow. The old faith will not die: the trunk of the grape vine you think long dry is even more laden than ever with grapes in autumn. Come, let us sit near the flickering hearth. Are you tired? Have patience. In my shelter it is warm.

(they take their place by the fire)

So, where were we? Ah, yes, "deception."

MAGUL

(brightening suddenly)

A thought, old one, a thought. Listen to me, I am not alone, after all. You are good for me, you have not abandoned me, have you? Shall we then spread a curse secretly among the people? Shall we give the people a ghost? Zalmoxis' religion is making itself a nest in the hearts of the most faithful through the old quarters. He hasn't returned, and yet he is here. He smashes our gods, for his Blind One. So, how would it be if we spread the story among the people that Zalmoxis, himself, was a god; what do we have to lose? For the price of one extra god in our gracious temple, we will save the whole pantheon of gods. Can you see it? As the people begin to worship Zalmoxis, they will soon forget his teaching.

SORCERER

A worthy curse from the wisdom of a mag. Of course! A legend, a maker of miracles. People will deify Zalmoxis — and they will forget his teaching! Is this your idea? O, great priest!

MAGUL

(suddenly suspicious)

There is no one else in the cottage? Is your door bolted shut?

SORCERER

Have no fear.

MAGUL

(with renewed cunning)

The field, my friend, is fresh, and the legend will stretch forth its roots. The people will shout "Let us place the statue of Zalmoxis in the temple among the other gods, as it becomes him." When there is no more strength left to harness a new prophet, a single thing is more powerful than the prophet himself: his statue! Give me your hand, and your thoughts in friendship.

SORCERER

(extending his hand)

My hand and my word!

MAGUL

(softly)

The water obeys you!

SORCERER

(more softly)

The fire obeys me!

MAGUL

The wind obeys you!

SORCERER

The stars obey me!

MAGUL

Above all things, even that which is not, obeys you.

SORCERER

I know how to bewitch stories, so that they become truth.

MAGUL

I gave you the story.

SORCERER

I will add the charm.

MAGUL

(jumps suddenly)

A deafening sound by the cottage!

SORCERER

'Tis nothing, old friend, but the footfall of silence — I hear nothing.

MAGUL

Their hatred tracks my scent! Just open the door and listen, you will hear it!

The sorcerer opens the door and lets out a shout.

SORCERER

The fortress is burning!

They both run out.

MAGUL

Fire in the south. Fear. The temple is far, but they will not overtake it. O, only that the sky should not burn. There are other flames — quiet, listen.

SORCERER

It is distant crying.

MAGUL

They have tracked me.

SORCERER

'Tis only frightened birds. They are shaking the soot and hot ash from their wings.

MAGUL

And the wind brings the ash up to here.

Both of them withdraw, shaken. The Sorcerer gives Magul a sign that he should hide in the cellar, near the hearth. Then the sorcerer puts kindling on the fires that is about to extinguish. After a few moments, the Shepherd appears. He is wearing a sheep skin coat, and has a sickly countenance.

SHEPHERD

Tomorrow the moon rises. I am afraid of her light. The sun is easy, but the moon is hard. When it touches my eyelids, I fall as though struck with a club on my forehead and I change into fireflies. No matter where I am, whether on the mountains, waiting on a ridge, or whistling in the sheepfold, I fall... and then... I transform into a black beast, and I... I tear up sheep from my own flock.

(sorrowfully)

I have heard from passersby that you have remedies for such afflictions. You can cure me of the moon.

SORCERER

Since when have you born this punishment?

SHEPHERD

It was during the seventh harvest of the vine. The crowd was uneasy, they had gathered in the orchard and were listening to Zalmoxis speaking the word of the Blind One.

(deep in recollection)

I was the first to hit him,

(raising his fingers to his face)

Here, in the cheek, I hit him with a rock. It was Magul — he teased us — Oh, I don't even know anymore. I trembled, I did — and afterward, I ached because the young man I struck with a rock opened his eyes wide and asked us "why?"

(momentarily lost)

The moon appeared that night. I ripped five sheep to shreds and then I wept in their fleece. Ever since then I take to the fields full speed the same way. I track the young man with big eyes, and seek the blood that runs from his body in the sand. After I sip a drop of his spilled blood, I come to my senses, and transform back into a man.

SORCERER

I will consult with a superior grace and weed out this mystery of Zalmoxis. You are not the first to suffer in his wake, stranger.

SHEPHERD

Guard me from the moon.

The sorcerer tosses nuggets of incense into the flames, and then raises his hand over the fire with great ceremony.

SORCERER

You, who sees through things, o, spirit of the hearth, ember of the twilight, reveal yourself to me in your language of the flames.

VOICE OF MAGUL

(from the cellar)

Zalmoxis wasn't a man.

SHEPHERD

Guard me from the moon.

VOICE OF MAGUL

Zalmoxis wasn't a man.

SORCERER

You see through things, and through hearts.

VOICE OF MAGUL

Zalmoxis wasn't a man, he was a god. He descended from the nest of eternity on stairs of light to teach you youth and pain, until you — you struck him so that even the rock cries out.

SORCERER

The deathless make their nest on a mountain that rises out of daybreak. Will not Zalmoxis return to his sky the same way?

VOICE OF MAGUL

He has no sanctuary, nothing carved in his image as would befit a god, no likeness to which the faithful may bow in worship. Zalmoxis is bound in clay. He will send dangers into your souls, and rocks will grind the earth while lambs will perish like the grapes off the vine. Carve him, therefore, a body, a body of stone for Zalmoxis! The god calls out; he asks for sacrifice.

The Sorcerer takes the skull from the hearth and moves it through the flames.

SORCERER

Show yourself, unseen spirit, in the murmur of the flames. Save the lunatic from his affliction, and cure his suffering, for in these drops of wine, the blood spilled from Zalmoxis has gather.

The sorcerer repeats this incantation two more times.

VOICE OF MAGUL

You are my master.

The shepherd, who has been listening the whole time in amazement, falls now to his knees. The sorcerer gives him the charmed drink from the skull.

SORCERER

Playing on the crests beneath the tall pines the moon will cross your path. And the moon will want to pour friendship into your soul — softly, sweetly, mildly, and tenderly. The sheep will fear you no longer, and neither will your dogs. This time bow down more virtuous than before to this god whom you struck. Bring trout upon his altar like a holy fisherman.

ACT II

Scene 1

An orchard surrounded by vineyards scattered on the hills. To the right of the orchard is a forest. Large earthen amphorae are filled with fermenting wine.

FIRST HARVESTER

This is the hunchback?

SECOND HARVESTER

Yes.

THIRD HARVESTER

Do you marvel at such wondrous fruit? The hunchback has his secret recipe: beneath every vine trunk he has buried a human corpse that he's found on the road or even in the water.

SECOND HARVESTER

Is it true that he knows how to charm the mice off the branches?

FIRST HARVESTER

Do not gaze upon him so: you'll rot your eyes out.

SECOND HARVESTER

Look at him. He is nothing but skin and bones and still he doesn't want to die.

THIRD HARVESTER

And he won't die all too soon, either. If his soul leaves him, he'll simply steal his neighbor's. With a stolen soul the miserable thief lives on another man's life.

The hunchback comes near them.

FIRST HARVESTER

(to the hunchback)

What a splendid harvest you have. Why then do you not bark a psalm of happiness, eh? Ha-u, ha-u.

HUNCHBACK

I have no one to thank for my harvest.

SECOND HARVESTER

How is that? Not even the dead buried beneath your grapevines?

HUNCHBACK

Why are you offended? Because they warm their blood in the shoots of my grapevines?

FIRST HARVESTER

Indeed. And from all this plenty you don't think to bring an offering to Zalmoxis?

HUNCHBACK

(sarcastically)

Ah, this new immortal of yours collected at long last from his travels? And when he was crawling around those poor folks he wanted to kill your gods... to cut his slippers from their skin. And now? Now you offer him sacrifices as well. Strange times! Yet why do they still chatter? All is well; from now on you have a god who finally understands your language. *(Ironically)* The others, after all, speak only Greek.

SECOND HARVESTER

You have a sharp tongue, Hunchback.

HUNCHBACK

(mean-spirited)

I cannot be otherwise, since my mother saw fit to give me a back thick enough for three, and not enough of a body for one. But let me grumble not; each man receives his own fate — mine, you see, I carry hidden in my hump.

(Gesturing toward the approaching shepherd)

While the fate of others are hidden in the moon… ha ha ha ha.

FIRST HARVESTER

(to the shepherd)

You are a saint.

SECOND HARVESTER

(meekly, to the shepherd)

Since you freed from dreams the tale of Zalmoxis, the god, there is peace in the fortress.

THIRD HARVESTER

You have reconciled the Mag with the new disciples and blood no longer runs.

SHEPHERD

I am waiting for the priestess to come, so we can go on together. Will you come also?

HARVESTERS ALL

We will come also!

SHEPHERD

And you will do anything for me?

FIRST HARVESTER

(falling to the ground)

For the one sent by Zalmoxis — anything! Say to me, "Drench your hair with sap" and if necessary, I would put a flame to my hair that you should have candle in the middle of the night. Say, too, "Throw yourself into the bramble" and if necessary I will sacrifice myself like a ripe quince that falls in the mud. Say, "Hurl yourself into the thorns" and tomorrow I would be pecked by the birds like a grape.

SHEPHERD

I want only this much: When I say yes, you say yes, too. When I say no, you say no, as well.

SECOND HARVESTER

You are a saint.

The three harvesters go into the vineyards. The shepherd sits on a bluff and begins to play a moving ode on a flute. Three children suddenly jump out from the woods, each one with a reed in hand. They foist themselves over the amphora filled with fermenting wine, and begin to suck through the reeds.

THE SMALLEST CHILD

(upset)

The juice is not coining through my reed!

THE OLDEST CHILD

It has knots in it. Go and choose another — you'll find plenty in the marsh.

THE SMALLEST CHILD

(beginning to cry)

I'm afraid of the leeches.

THE OLDEST CHILD

(annoyed)

Be quiet. Look there! The shepherd. He's coming to take you away.

THE MIDDLE CHILD

It's the shepherd who turns into a firefly at night.

THE SMALLEST CHILD

(yells with fright)

Where is he?

THE OLDEST CHILD

(consoles him)

Calm yourself, Nusitatu, you restless little boy. Close your eyes, so he can't see you. That's right, close them tight, and everything becomes dark so that no one can even glimpse you. Did you close them? There. Now it's night. No one sees you. You'll be all right, then, Nusitatu.

THE MIDDLE CHILD

(holding back his laughter)

Not even I can see you.

THE OLDEST CHILD

Not even the firefly can see you.

The two older boys resume drinking through their reeds, while the little one sits apart on the grass. He is squeezing his eyes shut. Laughter and yelling are heard as someone approaches. The shepherd stands up and listens.

A Harvester jumps out from the grapevines and grabs the children by the hands.

A HARVESTER

Hide yourselves, children! Beware the Bacchante, a single look from them and you will remain dwarfs!

The children hide themselves in the vines.

A group of bacchantes enter from the left, dancing wildly in the orchard. Their faces are green and their braids fly in the wind. Some of the bacchantes twirl snakes above their heads, like whips. Others blow in the horn of oxen. They make more whooping sounds and continue their wild dancing. The shepherd stands in the middle of the group.

The harvesters pour out of the vineyards. As if by some sign, the madness ceases all of a sudden.

In the greatest silence, a single bacchante dressed in white, scatters ashes from an urn.

A BACCHANTE

From this urn I spread ashes of the dead on the roads. Let the wind lift them, carry them toward the sea. The ashes of those who are no more, I now sprinkle upon the earth in your path, children, you, who haven't yet been born. From the horns of oxen — eha — we call you! Descend! All of you by the hands, you, infants, assume your destiny of clay. The udders of the world are full, catch them, wring them, toward today, you, unborn, flow toward today. A smell of death breezes through the pine, the sun suckles you. Pass through the ashes, for the grapes are children and the ground asks you, "are you on your way? e-ha, e-ho!"

The dance of the Bacchante starts anew. Unintelligible yelling, "ehove, ehove, ehove." The harvesters answer, "ehove, ehove!"

SHEPHERD

(keeping the dance's beat)

Nine green priestesses
jump through the woods and the orchard
They pass through flower beds with
bramble,
blood runs through the thistle, the
stars and the earth
butterfly with snakes in the wind,
over the stars and the earth.
They don't know the paths, they would
dance even in the bottom of the sea.
They shudder after their gods, making
mad in the valleys with yelling
everything that is dead and all that is alive.

A VOICE

Glory be to Zalmoxis.

THE BACCHANTES

Glory be to the god Zalmoxis!

HARVESTERS All

Glory!

Grapes fall from the vines and shower the dance of the Bacchantes. The mountains answer with echoes.

SHEPHERD

Let us go to the great Mag!

A BACCHANTE

Let us ask him to fulfill the dream!

SHEPHERD

Leave the harvest in the care of the ravens. Come, dance, Ehove, Zalmoxis.

All run toward the woods with him, shouting "Ehove, Ehove!"

Scene 2

The inside of Zalmoxis' cave. Night. Everything takes place as though in a world of ghosts, with a strange slowness of speech.

ZALMOXIS

(hidden in the darkness)

I have descended deeper and deeper into my soul. Where am I, where am I? Still in the cave?

Zalmoxis begins to emerge in full view.

My heart wants to jump out of my chest.

(He spreads his hands over his heart.)

He peers out.

I can see through the mountains; the fortress doesn't move, and yet we get closer from now.

(softly, as though an invocation)

A leaf falls in the night

He drops slowly to one knee.

a lifetime drains in me,

He sinks to the other knee

another leaf falls in the night,

He stretches out his hand.

another lifetime passes in me.

An apparition appears in a corner of the cave. An old man who holds in his hand a cup. The light is reflected off the image through the whole cave. Zalmoxis rises and steadies himself against the cave wall, approaching the apparition.

ZALMOXIS *(cont'd)*

Old Man, shall I whisper to you all of my anguish? *(He studies the ghost.)* One would think that you live, but I see your eyes don't blink. Where have you come from?

OLD MAN

From a place where time is not.

ZALMOXIS

Only dreams come from there.

OLD MAN

And great dreamers.

ZALMOXIS

What can you tell me?

OLD MAN

When you are a wellspring, you have no choice but to run towards the sea! You, Zalmoxis, why do you shelter yourself in this cave?

ZALMOXIS

I fear that too soon I will carry a new faith among people.

OLD MAN

Too soon? Never. Today or later — it matters not; the same gift greets you. Ah, Zalmoxis, life has no stars for us — hemlock grows on garbage. Why do you think this is so? In whose honor?

The Old Man brings the cup to his mouth, stops all at once, and then finishes with bitter irony.

I almost forgot. When you are the fate's host, it is fitting to give the gods any drink whatsoever. This time I will observe the custom and toast with them.

He spills drink on the ground.

Drink, you too, bright as rot. Drink, green juice of hemlock. A cup is too much for me.

He drinks what remains.

ZALMOXIS

And so would I toast with them, the same! But what fault do you tempt?

OLD MAN

Only one: doubt. I never doubted.

He vanishes.

ZALMOXIS

(alone)

Bitter secrets have I peeled open throughout my years whitened with wisdom. But not one traveler crossed my path that I might graft my answer to his heart. When the days arise on peaks, my hair is as flames to me, but no one is there, no one to see me struck, mortified upon the rocks.

(slowly, softly)

A leaf falls in the night,
a lifetime drains in me,
another leaf falls in the night,
another lifetime passes in me.

A young man appears with long braids and a crown of thorns on his head. Zalmoxis approaches him.

Answer me! Are you my fate?

YOUNG MAN

Oh, no, but just as good a friend. I bring you news from the other side, your moment draws near, new man, in this night all the figs ripen. The children wait for them.

ZALMOXIS

Have you come to shake them down?

YOUNG MAN

They fall open on their own. Do you not hear them?

ZALMOXIS

I hear it. Someone calls me to the world. I feel the breezes as if from a great death. But what do you want with your crown of thorns?

The young man removes the crown from his brow, breaks the thorns, and spreads them as if sowing.

YOUNG MAN

I am planting thorns beneath the Milky Way — and I am waiting for sorrow to grow forth, many sorrows.

He disappears.

ZALMOXIS

(alone)

I try in vain to catch you again, incomprehensible apparition. You free yourself but leave me to knead reprimands with my fists. Cave, cave! You have made my winters mild and leavened my past beneath your watch. Where are my wounded memories that you caressed till they were forgotten. Give them to me now, that I can be the rebel once again? Destiny awaits me, impatience chokes me. See how I tremble; I take my life in my hands and leave for the future, toward eternal tomorrow!

To you, cave, I leave but these tracks of hard heels, and if you want, a shout. A shout of victory. Or failure, perhaps — who can say which?

The dawn so resembles the dusk.

People, Zalmoxis the peaceful one reenters your passions. The world and the tree have molted beneath my eyes — and I have seen what is clotted in chaos — and what is the seed in any fruit fallen in the lap of time.

I have had my fill of the dream.

O, rocks, I have looked at you for so long, that I have made myself a rock as well. Now, vigorously I melt and spill my crazed self forth from my river bed towards the plains and the people.

(more quietly)

More ghosts appear today... travails that bite into the rock. Once the nights were a cradle of rest for me, while during the day the world around seemed to collect within me into a dream so peaceful, that — cold and damp — the lizards were crowding at my bare feet to find the sun.

(soft and quite)

a leaf falls in the night,
a lifetime drains in me,

another leaf falls in this night
another lifetime passes in me.

A man appears, on in years, tied to a stake. Zalmoxis stretches his arms toward him.

THE MAN ON THE STAKE

Did you call me?
I am but an echo of your nights.

ZALMOXIS

Is this true? If you and I kneeled on the edge of lake of the dead and of those who have not yet been born; if we looked into the lake as though it were a mirror, would we see that we are one in the same? Is this true?

THE MAN ON THE STAKE

The many times you look for yourself, you find me.

ZALMOXIS

Who has tied you to the stake?

THE MAN ON THE STAKE

The eternal balancer, the one who is always awake.

ZALMOXIS

I don't know him.

THE MAN ON THE STAKE

The eternal balancer is he who makes you pause, and think until you have exhausted that thought. He arrests you in the middle of the road, and chains you there, "Enough, fool!" He cries out to you, because, you see, a complete thought is a calamity. Yet I say to you, calamity? So it is! Rise up, mankind toward the sky, or else may the worms gnaw at you in the grave.

ZALMOXIS

And look, the balancer comes to light your stake, after all.

(a hand is seen with a torch, setting fire to the kindling)

THE MAN ON THE STAKE

But the earth hears while the earth forgets not.

He vanishes in flames.

ZALMOXIS

(alone, agitated)

My eyes are drunk with scenes more lifelike than these bald rocks. Answer, heart! Be strong, my hand! The Blind One asks a sacrifice of you. Should I pierce the earth like an eye of the sea? Shall I tear my body for a flock of starving people? Or should I take the sun upon my back and carry it down into the valleys, or even more than this?

Or should I leave a second time into the country that deceived me? Among the people?

Cave, I change you into a bugle of my departure.

(with a yell)

Come, Blind One, come — that I will build you a ford in the river toward the life of the people.

He storms out from the cave. A sea of light confronts him.

Scene 3

The middle of the night. A stretched out plain. Not one tree. The Milky Way is intensely visible. Not one hill. Magul and the Greek woodcarver walk about with old steps — stopping from time to time.

MAGUL

The harvesters and the priestesses have filled my courtyard asking for the new idol.

Have you started the statue of Zalmoxis?

WOODCARVER

I have been carving these seven nights.

MAGUL

How is the marble?

WOODCARVER

It is as transparent as the water when the sky falls into the bottom of the sea.

MAGUL

(showing the plains)

Here is the plain of the fireflies of fire. They burst into light from the rotting ground. And the footfall of the sad, and the poor head toward treasures hidden in the earth of dead Dacian kings.

WOODCARVER

(pointing to the sky)

Look: the Milky Way. Not even those who die can make them burn any more beautiful.

MAGUL

(raising his eyes)

What do the old Greek teachers say of her? She to whom the gods themselves go like disciples to learn — what the world is, and the meaning of a thought?

WOODCARVER

(stopping himself)

If I do not deceive myself, a bribe brought from across the sea says that the road of the sun wasn't always as today. His path crisscrosses that one, from this one here and now. The Milky Way is nothing more than stardust left on the crystal vault of heaven, a mere fingerprint of the sun from so many years ago that scarcely a mind might figure it out.

MAGUL

Traces of the sun on the road of eternity. A thrill pierces me.

(the distant sound of wailing women is heard)

WOODCARVER

Weeping women. Someone must have died.

MAGUL

No. A babe has been born.

WOODCARVER

One wails at the birth of a child! I have seen much of the world, known so many countries and still, I can tell you there isn't another people who consume their life like yours, High Priest! Yesterday I saw a game of young men jumping over a spear. They supported themselves with a pole and thus they flew — just like that — u-hai-hop! Then one of them torn open his belly on the spearpoint — and the others had begun to burst out laughing at his awkwardness. And yet, it had been only a game. It is like this: see how a lightening bolt is not a man — that's how little a Dacian is a man. He doesn't live. He is lived.

His strength is plucked from the grail cup of giant beings, he hasn't love for himself, nor love for others. At last I understood that everything is because it must be so.

(he catches Magul by the arm)

Stop yourself — don't trip. Your coat has caught on the thorns.

MAGUL

(avoiding the thorns)

Your word stirs in me a new dread.

WOODCARVER

You are tempted to think that Dacians are not born of man into man. Nature alone creates them, she herself, suddenly; like she makes herself mountains, or springs. Remember Zalmoxis? The unknown one who brought down from the mountain three things; wonder, storm, and law. You were an enemy to him — I understand you.

But he was a native Dacian.

When he advised through parables, he wasn't saying "live for others" or "be a man;" rather "be a spring," "be lightning." Isn't his blind god something other than this kind of being and that of the Dacians — wild, tormented, blind, strange, eternally tried? Oh, no. I don't feel myself enclosed by people, rather, I feel very much in the middle of nature, so much so that I wonder that they haven't tufts of moss on their heads instead of hair —like the rocks.

MAGUL

(slyly)

Yes, the memory carries me to Zalmoxis, the woodsman. Yet the blameless flock has so distorted him that today he wouldn't know himself.

WOODCARVER

Believe me, with their hearts they understood him and even now, are close to him. But Dacians have the imagination of children.

MAGUL

If he would live like Zalmoxis urged them to, they would consume themselves like fire. Children need a gentle dream to calm them — and light to stop them from bolting, to hold back forces that swarm in their earth made too fertile by troubled wellsprings.

WOODCARVER

If it would be a question of peace, I give you the right, High Priest. But why peace?

MAGUL

A question which I answer with another question: Why a blind storm?

WOODCARVER

(hesitating)

I don't know.

MAGUL

Nor do I.

(fearful)

And still, I stop myself. You are strange and see perhaps better than I. I am cold. Come, maestro, it is late.

WOODCARVER

You would think that the coolness would descend slowly from the Milky Way, like a giant river. Come, the fortress is not far.

(they go toward the right)

Did you ever think, Magul... Magul, what would it be like if Zalmoxis returned one day — a man?

MAGUL

(decidedly)

He would perish, or the people would.

WOODCARVER

Or he and the people, both.

ACT III

Scene 1

A hill with a precipice of red clay and a curling stream of water from a wellspring. On the left, towers and walls of the fortress. On the right starts the forest of oak. In the foreground an orchard with tall grass and rocks. The thick of morning. Much sun.

The Woodcarver is sitting on a rock beneath an oak. White braids on his shoulders. He is creating a small human likeness out of clay. He is whistling. Zemora, young and wild, thistles in her unbraided hair, creeps in from the forest behind the woodcarver and tickles his braids with a long blade of grass.

WOODCARVER

(Raises his brow, but doesn't turn. He guesses.)

Zemora — the daughter of Magul, or perhaps a locust?

ZEMORA

One or the other. Because the wild Zemora loves the grass and the sun, alive like the locusts and she would want to have legs so green, green like the locusts or the pods of marshes.

WOODCARVER

Did you know you would find me — here?

ZEMORA

I saw your footprints in the clay as I climbed the path. Like so, in a row. I was thinking first that they are the tracks of... a donkey.

(she laughs)

Do you hear the forest? Only I know how to make it laugh.

(laughing heartily)

Do you hear how it laughs? Like a little child when you tickle his belly button.

WOODCARVER

(nodding his head)

Zemora, Zemora!

ZEMORA

What are you creating out of clay?

WOODCARVER

A figure of Zalmoxis.

ZEMORA

I heard Zalmoxis speak many times, though I didn't understand too much of what he spoke. But his eyes were so big, that I had to stop and listen to him. One time I was meeting him here somewhere in the forest, alone. He struggled to catch a swarm of bees that hovered over a branch like a nest. He was sealing the bottom of a straw basket with bees wax, when I jumped out into the road. "Zalmoxis," I said to him, "you are very young, and I am beautiful, but do not be afraid. I will teach you how to catch the swarm, and you, you will tell me about the beginning of the world, for in this you understand better than anyone."

He stirred. I took the basket from his hand, and I propped it upon a pole over the swarm, like a hat. He watched quietly. Then I smoked the bees by lighting a tinder with flint strikes — and they began to hide in the wicker covering. When I finished, I told him "Promise, eternal young woodsman!" He enfolded me with his eyes that were like caves filled with smiles, yet sad, and sweet, too.

He whispered to me, "Oh, I must tell you something, but you will not understand it with your mind — rather with your wild beauty.

I don't know. Am I dreaming? It seems that the Blind One created woman in the same day that he also created the moon."

WOODCARVER

Maybe from one and the same awesome light. Twin beings.

ZEMORA

Afterwards, Zalmoxis ran into the forest. He forgot the swarm there... but on the fourth day bad luck followed from this orchard.

WOODCARVER

(he offers her the small figure of clay)

Zemora, tell me, does this resemble your bee-catcher?

ZEMORA

(looking closely at the figure)

Zalmoxis was too much to behold, while this is too much man.

(flatteringly)

A gift for Zemora, yes?

WOODCARVER

(taking his figure)

No. It is for a house altar.

ZEMORA

For a house altar? Whose?

WOODCARVER

The great leader. Have you forgotten that tomorrow is the holiday in honor of all the unknown gods?

(he rises to leave)

ZEMORA

Do you want to leave?

WOODCARVER

I am going home to polish the statue of Zalmoxis some more, the one of marble. Where are you going?

(he takes a lump of clay in his arms)

ZEMORA

Up there, to dry my sandals in the sun. They are damp with dew.

WOODCARVER

Still to the sun, always to the sun?

ZEMORA

Ever toward the sun and the forest!

The woodcarver disappears on the path off to the left, while Zemora goes off into the woods. Pause. Birds singing.

In another part of the forest Zalmoxis arrives in the illuminated orchard. A club in his hand and soot in his beard.

ZALMOXIS

The orchard where they struck me. The paths are the same.

Fortress, are you here? My eyelids struggle with your sky, like butterflies against a window. It's not just a tale? Am I here?

(he feels a tree with his hand)

I feel the sharp bark of the tree and feel I am really here. Like a ripe fruit I broke myself from a branch of a god... and fall here, on the threshold of your fortress!

VOICE OF ZALMOXIS

Where is your stake?

ZALMOXIS

Are you waiting for me? Have you another friend for me?

VOICE OF ZALMOXIS

Where are your thorns? With what hands will you receive the sun that I will bring down for you from the peaks, like a gift in the light. Babes of birch grow on the walls — a sign that you did not exhaust yourself in great battles since you left, crazy people.

ZALMOXIS

You've had plenty of time to cast your nets in the multitude of eternity.

Did you fish worries from bottomless waters? Maybe you have burned your gods a long time ago. Have you crumbled your altars with the heads of oxen?

VOICE OF ZALMOXIS

My hope is ever wide-eyed toward the future. I believe many things. I am patient.

ZALMOXIS

The orchard where they struck me. The stray dogs of shepherds licked the blood that dripped from me on their way over the stony path. A sign that today you love me — oh, fortress? A sign that tomorrow you will raise a temple to the Blind One?

However it will be, however heavy with life, even with the thought of death I hurl my destiny into your walls, secret fortress. The mountains come with me.

He stops and listens. A song is heard from the oak forest.

VOICE OF ZEMORA

I wander toward the sun —

from the trembling greenery,

he falls in my harp that I

I know not how to sing anymore.

The bald horizon. My thought is stupid to me; a white rose calls me and I take the road to the grove. Thorns dig into my hand. The snakes pass through the twilight, and blood drips from wounds upon the strings. And the strings come together to sing into the night's ear. Drops fall together over old secrets.

Zemora reappears in the orchard with a bouquet of flowers.

ZALMOXIS

The first man. After seven years how comforting to my sight is the first man I behold.

He draws nearer to Zemora.

My lady — as fresh as autumn mornings — what song do you sing?

ZEMORA

You are a stranger to these parts, for the shepherds have long played it on their flutes, while the bard Madura made up the words.

ZALMOXIS

I used to know him — a long time ago. Is he still alive? Did he die?

ZEMORA

He lived for a long time in his own little fortress, all alone, until his soul had murdered him. No one knows why. People say that one night they had heard silver hoofbeats on the road below. Roads are like guitars — the older they are, the more beautiful they sound. And then, an auburn stallion galloped out of the moon dust without a rider in the saddle and made for the castle at breakneck speed. But tied to his tail a harp dragged at the end of a rope, like a dead man.

ZALMOXIS

Alas, that is how Dacian bards die.

ZEMORA

(affected)

Are you not saddened by the bitter laughter of one who no longer wants to turn back to life, and instead sends his horse back alone? And do you not see the auburn horse whipped into a frenzy by falling stars? On the road below a harp drags behind him like a dead man.

ZALMOXIS

I understand Madura all too well.

(suddenly pleading)

Will you grant me another question? The flowers — who are they for?

ZEMORA

I am taking them to the temple. Why not take a rest there from your travels, stranger. The holiday begins at dawn. The people are going to dedicate a statue of the god Zalmoxis in the sanctuary. I will make an offering of honey in his name, as well. When he was among us, I taught him how to catch swarms of bee.

Zemora leaves, smiling. Zalmoxis remains dumbfounded, staring toward the fortress.

Scene 2

An alleyway behind the fortress. Night. The moon is shining.

Zalmoxis passes with his head bowed.

ZALMOXIS

The mountain birds are singing. But where are my friends? I cannot find them. Bramble has overgrown their orchards and grass now covers their hearths. Be still, my heart! I can hear the rush of a waterfall in the valley, or perhaps it is only the breeze of the river of the dead.

VOICE OF ZALMOXIS

And here is my shadow, too. I have never understood it. I cast it from me, and still it is greater than I am.

ZALMOXIS

Breezes from the river of the dead, and again sing the mountain birds. Oh my heart — be silent!

He disappears. The Hunchback tails quickly behind him.

Scene 3

The temple. A lateral wall represents the foundation. The six principle gods are arranged in a horseshoe, on pedestals. One is larger than the rest, and has the head of a bull. The sacrificial altar is in the center. One pedestal is empty. Two tall brass-colored pillars support the vault. The temple entrance is to the right, but unseen. Sacrifices and rows of small graven images are along the back wall. A vague light reflects from the above. Candles burn on the altars and in the sacrificial motives. The temple is empty.

Zalmoxis enters stage right. His eyes are bright. He stops near the column in front. The sound of voices calling can be heard in the distance.

ZALMOXIS *(cont'd)*

The masses are gathered in my name. I walked past them, and they looked at me with strange eyes — people forget. No one remembers me anymore. Their joyful clatter would lift me to the heavens, but without my teaching. The smell of wine sprays me. How cold are these tombstones.

Magul comes out of the altar in white vestments and notices the stranger while putting incense in the votive candles.

MAGUL

You there, stranger. How dare you? Did you not fear to cross this threshold before the statue of Zalmoxis has been dedicated? No one among the profane would not take such liberties.

Zalmoxis is silent. Magul draws nearer, he looks into Zalmoxis' eyes and reacts with remembrance.

MAGUL *(cont'd)*

O, the troubled gaze of these eyes, so changed. And here? Here again? And today of all days? Zalmoxis, I know you;

(choking as though strangled)

but why have you returned? Why have you come back? The people are rioting without wanting, without knowing why.

(with mean laughter)

You tried to wean them from statues, and yet today, you will have a stone carved in your image among them!

ZALMOXIS

(laughing)

And you! You are my priest! Unbelievable! What a blasphemous rebellion!

MAGUL

So young were you when you sowed that seed, yet you did not expect such a fruit to flower. It is difficult to change now. You surely reap what you sow from a field, but from the human heart, the same is not true. Here you plant wheat, and cherries grow.

(flatteringly)

Otherwise, are you not pleased? All of these bronze-colored columns stand like slender young maids who have cast off their robes and dance all around you. An altar have you, and people to fall on their knees in the dust for you.

(bitterly)

Leave, then! The altar has no steps! You are high above us — but in vain you search — for you can never descend again. Rebellion? Against whom? Today you have no enemies left, the people worship you — and I, I am your priest!

ZALMOXIS

Indeed you are my priest! Ha-Ha! But I will not leave this place. I will hurl myself upon this tombstone. I will seize the lightning in my clenched fists!

MAGUL

O, your god is blind — and you, poor youth, have taken fate upon your shoulders.

ZALMOXIS

And this fate makes me strike out.

MAGUL

The people will not believe it is you. And strike out? At whom? Have you an enemy? I think not — except perhaps time, yes, time who has set stone upon stone and raised a temple for you — damnation upon it!

ZALMOXIS

I will turn back time with whips of lighting, and tomorrow will be today! I will call out from the deep of my terminal shores, and time will turn back like the sea when the moon beckons it. And then I will draw close to your ear and whisper "make haste, old undertaker, and bury your gods the sky is full of rotting corpses!"

MAGUL

You are young... and blind. You come back a second time — why? You chose not to remain among us, so why have you returned? Go away, leave us!

Or stay. Are you hungry? Had you anything to eat in your little hideaway all those years? What suffering. I melt out of compassion for you. You are thin. Go! But when the days shrink with cold and hunger gnaws at you, you allow yourself to return from time to time, unknown, like a searcher; you should stand on the steps of these posts so that you can stretch your trembling hand to those who pass by. You will find, I am certain, people who will give you a crust of bread and drop of wine from their overripe harvest. Likewise from my patience you will receive the remains left over from your altar. Tears of patience have I for you, Zalmoxis. O, do not try the fury of your people a second time. I am not evil, but you should make your way from here. You can always come back as a seeker, here upon the steps of the temple when you are hungry, and the snowstorm will warm beneath your ragged cloak.

Zalmoxis shakes so with emotion that he must steady himself against a column. He is overcome by the shouts of the multitude who approach the temple: "Ehove, ehove, Zalmoxis!" The shepherd and another Dacian carry the statue of Zalmoxis on their shoulders and set it down on the empty pedestal.

Many people gather, yet where Zalmoxis is standing there is no one beside him. The people sing constantly.

CHORUS OF CHILDREN

We carried your carved image through the alley ways, and had fallen naked on the sand. Are we not small and good? And are there not all those many swallows beneath the eaves who made their nests of clay, so short and sacred? O, do not disturb them now. For our sake, Zalmoxis, the god who was struck, have patience with those who took aim at you with slingshots filled with nuts. Please, do not damn those who hide from your face, and especially the kid-goats — guard them against the steep ridges and deep ravines, you — o, so awesome, so misunderstood!

MAGUL

(in front of the statues)

Raise the white statue of wet dust and holy wine upon the altar! Fall to your knees, fall down!

The people kneel. Magul raises his arms in supplication to the statue.

MAGUL *(cont'd)*

Turn back, Zalmoxis, toward the first masters of thoughts, of furrows, of light, and of the waters. The stars resound in echoes beneath the sandals of your ascent. Raise the threshold of eternity and caress these sad people with your prophetic hand.

Kneel, kneel! It is the day of all your sorrows. You have thrown sand in the eyes of the sun. Forgiveness! Weep, all of you and fill the temple with the scent of your tears! Arise, Zalmoxis!

VOICE OF THE PEOPLE

Arise, Arise, Arise!

Magul moves to the altar unseen.

MAGUL

Come out, maidens, all. Begin the sacred dance.

Six maids led by Zemora come in front of the divine statues. Each one bows down in turn to each of the six statues.

THE FIRST MAID

May cold ripples of gold be your mate, o, powerful bull.

THE SECOND MAID

My eyes are sweet and my body flutters in flight like flower petals in your sight.

THE THIRD MAID

Flower and man in mud worship you — the fire on the altar spreads its mist in me.

THE FOURTH MAID

I fill the moon with nuggets of incense, may undying embers remain in her for you.

THE FIFTH MAID

A horn of smoke climbs toward you. May hearts and dance always be your neighbors.

ZEMORA

(at the statue of Zalmoxis)

I offer you honey in ash and ember, to you, eternal beekeeper of the forest!

The dance of the maids begins, joined by guitars from the altar. Meanwhile...

Zalmoxis is still beside the column, having watched on with worry.

ZALMOXIS

They smother me; these cold winds twist and make me tremble from the base of heaven, for is not my body the sky? But the stars, green poison drips from them into my cup as though from the crushed heads of snakes... the very stars that I once loved, seem so bitter to me now.

I — a god? My faith has tempted you — thousands of naive worshippers! My fists make ready for battle! The enemy?

VOICE OF ZALMOXIS

It is you —

ZALMOXIS

It is you — you alone, only you, a chiseled image in stone crowned with immortality, and corrupted with the dances of young maidens.

He stretches out his arms in supplication.

ZALMOXIS

Zalmoxis, god, how white you are... like snow. But my dream is warm and I will melt you. Here I am with my human thought.

VOICE OF ZALMOXIS

And there?

ZALMOXIS

I... the god, and all the drunkards such sacrifice ordains. Statue! with your mountainous burden, lift me to your bosom. Damnation, slayer of dreams! Behold; I rise before you — do you not tremble, then? The swallows will make their nests in your head! Zalmoxis! god, if I should see you in the bramble, or in a dung heap, may the dogs bark about you to the moon. Like ashes in the wind — may you be scattered in the mud, your followers beside you. And time, I command you turn back like the sea — turn back, I say!

He hurls himself on his statue, and brings it crashing down with his fists. The people kneeling all around look on with confusion. They stand. There is chaos, and shouting, "Statue," "The god," "Broken," "Violated altar," "Woe," "Kill him." A couple of shepherds rush over to Zalmoxis and throw him over. They pelt him viciously with broken pieces of his statue. The Hunchback emerges from the crowd. He hurries beside the dead Zalmoxis and then turns harshly to the crowd.

HUNCHBACK

This is the second time he has come among you and you did not recognize him. He has eyes unlike any other, and yet, you knew him not. Come closer. Behold him! You have murdered Zalmoxis with his own statue, scoundrels!

There is amazement and a few gasps. Everyone gathers around the body, and then total silence.

FIRST BYSTANDER

Zalmoxis is dead.

SECOND BYSTANDER

But he brought us God.

FIRST BYSTANDER

The Blind One is among us once more.

SECOND BYSTANDER

And within us.

CURTAIN